SEBASTIAN
IN CENTRAL PARK

By M.C. Hall
Illustrated by David T. Wenzel

bear&
company™

Published by Bear & Company Publications
Copyright © 2002 by Bear & Company

Printed in the United States of America

Suitcase Bear Adventures™ is a registered trademark of Bear & Company.

Based on a series concept by Dawn Jones
Edited by Dawn Jones
Designed by Valerie Hodgson

Library of Congress Cataloging-in-Publication Data

Hall, Margaret, 1947-
Sebastian in Central Park / written by M.C. Hall ; illustrated by
David T. Wenzel.
p. cm. – (Suitcase bear adventures ; 1)
Summary: On a trip to New York City with his human family, a teddy bear
gets lost in Central Park and meets a new friend who helps him to find
them at the zoo.

ISBN 0-9713174-0-2 (alk. paper)
[1. Teddy bears–Fiction. 2. Dogs–Fiction. 3. Central Park (New York,
N.Y.)–Fiction.] I. Wenzel, David T., 1950- ill. II. Title. III. Series.
PZ7.H14625 Sg 2001
[Fic]–dc21
2001005173

To my mother and all her bears

M. C. Hall

Message to Parents

Bear & Company,

part of The Boyds Collection, Ltd. family,

is committed to creating quality reading and play

experiences that inspire kids to learn, imagine, and explore

the world around them. Working together with

experienced children's authors, illustrators, and educators,

we promise to create stories and products that are

respectful to your children and that will

earn your respect in turn.

Table of Contents

Chapter One
Skyscrapers and Elevators

"Those buildings look like mountains!" Sebastian said as he looked out the window. He was snuggled between Emily and her brother, Ben, in the back of a taxi.

"They're called skyscrapers," said Emily. "New York City is full of them."

Emily, Ben, and Sebastian belonged to one another. Emily Parker was nine years old. Ben was seven. They both had sandy hair and eyes the color of chocolate drops.

Sebastian had dark-brown hair and eyes the color of licorice drops. He wasn't sure how old he was.

Sebastian was a bear—a stuffed bear.

But Sebastian was real to Emily and Ben—and to anyone who really paid attention. Grown-ups didn't, Sebastian had found. They were too busy.

"Here we are, children," said a voice from the front seat. The voice belonged to Arabella Valentine. Ms. Valentine was a tall, thin woman with wild, curly hair and pale-blue eyes. She took care of the Parker children.

"Is this our hotel?" Ben asked as they got out of the cab.

"Yes," said Ms. Valentine. "Your parents are already here. We'll be right next door to them."

Mr. and Mrs. Parker traveled a lot. That was why they had hired Arabella Valentine. They wanted their children to be with them. But they didn't want them to miss too much schoolwork. So Ms. Valentine was part nanny and part teacher.

They walked into the hotel. Emily carried Sebastian in one hand and her suitcase in the other. Ben carried his suitcase and Sebastian's.

"Please wait here," said Ms. Valentine. "I'll get the key to our suite."

"Our sweet?" Sebastian whispered. "We have

Emily carried Sebastian in one hand and her suitcase in the other.

candy in our room?"

"No, silly," said Emily. "A suite is rooms that connect. It's spelled differently."

"Oh," said Sebastian, who wasn't a very good speller. He was a bit disappointed, because he loved candy.

Ms. Valentine returned, then led the way into the elevator. "Benjamin, you may push the button for the twentieth floor," she said.

Ben pushed, and the elevator zoomed upward. Sebastian watched the numbers above the door: 16 . . .17. . . 18 . . . 19 . . .

A bell dinged, and the elevator doors whooshed open. A minute later, Ms. Valentine had unlocked a door along a corridor.

"Ooh," said Sebastian when he and Emily entered. "This is nice. I think I like suites."

"So do I," Ben agreed. "Come on, Sebastian, let's check it out." He snatched Sebastian from his sister's arms.

"Hey!" Emily cried.

"I just want to show him the view," said Ben.

"No fighting, children," Ms. Valentine warned.

Ben rushed to a tall window at the far end of the

room. Emily was close behind.

"Look, Sebastian," said Ben. "You can see almost the whole city!"

"Why are there toy cars down there?"

"They're not toys," Emily explained. "They look little because we're up so high."

Ms. Valentine joined them. "Now, Benjamin," she said, "you know those aren't toys."

"It wasn't–"

Emily's elbow in his ribs made Ben stop before he could say that it was Sebastian she had heard. "I was just kidding," he muttered.

"Look over there, children," said Ms. Valentine. "Do you see all those trees? That's Central Park."

"Can we go there?" Ben asked.

"Yes," Ms. Valentine promised. "We'll be here for two whole days before we leave for London. Central Park is the last thing on our schedule."

"I can't wait," Sebastian whispered into Ben's ear.

"You'll have to," said Ben. "Ms. Valentine has a schedule, you know."

"I know," Sebastian sighed.

Chapter Two
Breakfast for a Bear

Sebastian slipped out of bed. Emily and Ben were sound asleep. The door to Ms. Valentine's room was still closed. But Sebastian had had enough sleep.

Still wearing his pajamas, Sebastian went into the living room of the suite. He looked out the window. He could see Central Park. And today was the day they were going there!

Then Sebastian realized that his tummy was rumbling. *I'm hungry*, he realized.

The night before, after they had returned from sight-seeing, Ms. Valentine had ordered dinner.

Sebastian had watched carefully. So now he knew what to do. He climbed up on a chair and reached for the telephone. With one paw, he pushed a button.

"Good morning. This is Room Service. How may we help you?" said a voice.

"Pancakes with honey, please," Sebastian said.

"Very well, sir," said the voice. "Will that be one order?"

Sebastian thought for a minute. He was *very* hungry. "Three orders," he said, "with extra honey."

As Sebastian hung up, he heard Ms. Valentine in the next room. "Rise and shine, children!" she said cheerfully.

Sebastian climbed down, tiptoed to the door, and peeked in. Emily and Ben were yawning and rubbing their eyes. "Time to shower and get dressed," Ms. Valentine was saying. "And then pack your suitcases. We'll be sending them on to the airport. Remember, we leave for London this evening."

Sebastian pulled the door shut. Everyone would be busy for a while. Meanwhile, he had breakfast to think about.

Just then, there was a knock at the door. "Come in," Sebastian called.

The door opened, and a young man stood there with a cart. A delicious smell floated into the room—warm pancakes drenched in honey.

The man looked around. The door to the bath was closed, and he heard water running. "Well, I'll just set things up," he said.

He pushed the cart inside. He unfolded napkins, uncovered three plates, and arranged silverware. He moved a chair up to the cart, then looked around again. "Breakfast is served," he said. He shrugged and headed out the door.

Sebastian piled two cushions on the chair and climbed up on top. He took a few deep breaths. There was nothing quite like the smell of warm pancakes.

Soon one plate was empty. Then another. Sebastian was almost through with the third plate when Emily and Ben came into the room.

Honey dripping from his snout, Sebastian smiled a sticky smile. No one smiled back.

"Sebastian!" Emily cried.

"Ms. Valentine is going to be so mad!" Ben said.

"You shouldn't have ordered from room service!" Emily scolded.

"But I was hungry," explained Sebastian.

"Stop eating right now!" Emily ordered. "We've got to get rid of this mess."

Sadly, Sebastian put down his fork.

"Open the door," Emily told Ben. "I'll push the cart out into the hall." In a matter of minutes, the cart was gone. So was the last pancake—uneaten.

Just then, Ms. Valentine walked in. "Let's order some breakfast," she said. "Oatmeal, milk, and juice–that's what growing children need."

"Growing bears need pancakes," whispered Sebastian.

"Did you say pancakes, Emily?" Ms. Valentine asked. "Nonsense! Pancakes need syrup. And syrup is bad for your teeth." Then she spoke into the phone. "Yes. We would like breakfast for three. Oatmeal, juice, and milk. Yes, this is Room 2012. No, there was no problem with our first order. This *is* our first order."

She put down the phone. "Odd," she said. "They must have us mixed up with another room."

"That's strange," said Emily, trying not to smile.

"Very strange," Ben added. He winked at Sebastian.

Chapter Three
Off to Central Park!

An hour later, they climbed out of another cab.

"Well," said Ms. Valentine, "our suitcases are on their way to the airport. And we have a whole day to spend in Central Park. You know, children, this was the first landscaped park in the country. That's why it's an important place to see."

"I thought it was important because it was fun," whispered Sebastian.

"That, too," Emily said with a smile.

"Now, let me check our schedule," Ms. Valentine continued. She unzipped her shoulder bag and pulled out a crisp sheet of paper.

"Can we go in now?" Ben asked. "Please?"

"All in good time," said Ms. Valentine. "I must check our schedule first. We need a plan so we can see as much as possible by 5 o'clock. That's when we meet your parents at the zoo."

Ben sighed a tiny little sigh. Sebastian could understand. Ms. Valentine liked to plan every-thing. Sometimes it was hard for small boys and bears to be patient with all that planning.

Ms. Valentine studied the paper, then nodded with satisfaction. At last, she folded it carefully and returned it to her shoulder bag. "The first thing on our list is Cleopatra's Needle," she announced.

"Who is Cleopatra?" asked Ben.

"I believe Emily can tell you," said Ms. Valentine.

"She was a queen in Egypt a long, long time ago," said Emily.

"Excellent," said Ms. Valentine. "However, Cleopatra actually had nothing to do with the needle." She turned and marched down the sidewalk.

As the children followed, Sebastian asked

Emily, "Why is there a needle in the park? And if it isn't Cleopatra's, whose is it?"

"I have no idea," said Emily. "But I'll bet Ms. Valentine knows."

"Knows what, Emily?" asked Ms. Valentine.

"Why it's called Cleopatra's Needle."

"Certainly," said Ms. Valentine. "It's called that just because the name Cleopatra makes people think of Egypt. And the needle came from Egypt. It stood in front of a temple there more than 1,000 years ago. Then someone bought it and gave it to the city of New York as a gift."

"Wow, that was some gift," said Ben. "Look at it!" He waved one hand toward the tall, pointed tower that had just come into view.

When they reached the base of the stone monument, Sebastian leaned back to see the top. He leaned so far that he almost slipped out of Emily's backpack. So he grabbed something to save himself.

"Ouch!" cried Emily. "My hair!"

"Benjamin, leave your sister alone," Ms. Valentine said without turning around.

"But . . .," spluttered Ben.

13

"It wasn't Ben," Emily said quickly. "I caught my hair on something." She sat down and helped Sebastian get out.

"This tower is magnificent," Ms. Valentine was saying as she studied Cleopatra's Needle. "Look carefully, children, and you can see Egyptian symbols carved into the stone."

They all moved closer, but the symbols were hard to see. Soon Sebastian gave up. He walked around to the other side. "It's not that high," he said to himself. "Not for a good climber like me."

Sebastian grabbed hold with all four paws and started inching his way upward. Soon he was four feet off the ground. Then he made the mistake of looking down. He froze–afraid to move in either direction.

A little girl shouted, "Look, Daddy! There's a bear on Cleopatra's Needle. Is it an Egyptian bear?"

The next voice Sebastian heard was Ms. Valentine's. "Really, Emily! You know better. Get your bear immediately!"

As soon as Emily reached for him, Sebastian let go and tumbled into her arms. "You saved me!" he cried.

He froze—afraid to move in either direction.

Emily hugged him. Then she frowned. "Sebastian, you're getting me in trouble again," she said.

"I don't mean to," said Sebastian.

"Come along, children," said Ms. Valentine. "We'll rent bicycles now. The park is enormous, and we can see more if we ride."

She led the way to a stall where a man rented them three bicycles. Emily helped Sebastian into her backpack carrier, and they all took off.

Ms. Valentine led the way. Ben followed her. Emily and Sebastian were last.

"Go faster!" Sebastian shouted. He loved riding with Emily. He loved the wind in his fur. He loved the way everything looked blurry as they went past.

"I'm going as fast as I can," Emily called.

Soon they stopped beside a large pond. "We'll rest here," Ms. Valentine said. "You might see some turtles if you look carefully."

"Neat!" said Ben. "Can I keep one?"

"Absolutely not," said Ms. Valentine. She sat down on a bench and pulled out her schedule.

Emily put Sebastian down on the grass. "Now,

you be good," she warned. Then she followed
Ben, who was headed toward the pond.

"I will," said Sebastian. He followed Emily.

Sebastian looked carefully, but he didn't see any
turtles. Just lots and lots of rocks. He stepped on
one, then hopped to another. *This is fun*, he
thought.

At least it was fun until Emily shouted,
"Sebastian–watch out!"

Sebastian was startled. He wobbled, then
slipped. As he slid off the rock, he noticed that it
had a head. And a wide-open mouth. The rock
was a huge turtle. And it looked like it wanted a
bite of Sebastian for lunch!

Chapter Four
Sebastian Takes a Tumble

Suddenly, Sebastian was lifted into the air. The turtle angrily snapped shut its mouth. Then it disappeared into the water.

"You saved me again!" cried Sebastian, throwing his paws around Emily's neck.

"Sebastian, you've got to stop finding trouble," said Emily.

"I think trouble finds me," said the bear.

Emily kissed one of Sebastian's ears. "I know," she sighed. "Now, get back up in my pack, where you belong. And stay there."

"I will," said Sebastian. "I promise."

"Ben, Emily!' called Ms. Valentine. "We have to keep moving or we'll never see everything!"

"Where are we going now?" Ben asked.

"To Belvedere Castle," said Ms. Valentine. "Follow me!"

They took off, riding quickly along the paved path. Sebastian shut his eyes, remembering his close call. He didn't think he liked turtles very much at all.

The sun was warm and the path was smooth, so Sebastian almost fell asleep. Then Emily's bike came to a stop. Sebastian's eyes popped open at once. He could see a huge stone castle, complete with a tower.

"Wow!" Sebastian exclaimed. "Does a king live there?"

"I don't think there are any kings in Central Park," Emily answered.

With Ms. Valentine in the lead, they started to explore. First they walked around the outside of the castle. Then they climbed a lot of steps. At last, they were as high as they could go. "Look at the view," said Ms. Valentine. "You can even see the lake."

"I'm going to use a telescope," said Ben. He put a quarter in the slot and aimed the telescope at the lake.

Sebastian pulled his binoculars out of his backpack. He looked through them for a few minutes. Somehow, they didn't seem as exciting as a telescope.

"I want to see," Sebastian told Emily.

Emily helped him down. "There you go," she said. She dropped a quarter into the slot and held Sebastian up to a telescope.

"It's like magic!" Sebastian said as he peered through the lens. "Everything is so close!"

"It just seems that way," Emily explained. "May I look now?"

Emily lifted Sebastian down to the floor. He stood there, wondering what to do. Everyone was busy with a telescope. Everyone but Sebastian. He turned around in a circle. Maybe he could climb up the tower.

No, he decided. *No more climbing. I promised Emily I'd be good.*

A few moments later, Ms. Valentine said, "Well, there is more to the castle than the view, children. There is a nature observatory inside. I certainly don't want you to miss that. So come along now."

Ben grabbed Sebastian. They followed Ms. Valentine down the stairs, through a door, and into a room filled with interesting displays.

"This is neat!" said Ben. He put Sebastian down and began to study some snakeskins.

"Ugh," Sebastian said. He looked for Emily. She was bending over a microscope while Ms. Valentine gave her instructions.

That looks like fun, Sebastian thought. He climbed up onto a chair by another microscope. He wasn't sure what to do, so he peeked over at Emily.

He saw her pull out a hair and put it under the microscope. Then she turned a knob.

Sebastian pulled out a tuft of brown fur and put it under the microscope. But when he bent down to look, the fur blew away.

He pulled out a little more fur and tried again. He was on his third try when Emily came over.

"What are you doing?" she asked.

"Trying to see my fur under the microscope."

"Your fur?" Emily repeated. Then she looked at Sebastian's head. "You'll be bald if you keep going!"

Sebastian lifted a paw to his head. Emily was right. He had pulled out more fur than he'd realized.

Ben and Ms. Valentine came over just as Emily picked Sebastian up. "It's time to go," said Ms. Valentine. "We have to stay on schedule."

They went back to their bikes and started off, riding past the lake. Emily pedaled faster and faster, trying to keep up.

Ms. Valentine is always in such a hurry, thought Sebastian. *She should slow down. There's so much to see!*

From his perch on Emily's back, Sebastian was busy looking at everything. On one side, there was a blur of blue water. On the other, in-line skaters and kids on scooters whizzed by.

Then Sebastian heard a tinkling sound. He knew what it meant—an ice cream truck! Suddenly, he realized how hungry he was. He pulled himself up and twisted around to tap Emily on the shoulder. He had to tell her that he needed ice cream, and maybe could she please try to get Ms. Valentine to stop?

Just then, Emily hit a bump. The bike went up in the air—then down with a thump. It tipped, but didn't fall.

Sebastian wasn't as lucky. He tumbled toward the path.

Chapter Five
More Close Calls

"Stop!" shouted Sebastian as he flew through the air. But Emily kept going.

Sebastian landed with a thud. *It's a good thing I'm stuffed*, he thought. *Otherwise, I could have been hurt.*

Just then, a skateboard whizzed by, narrowly missing Sebastian. The little bear rolled off the path and out of danger.

That was close, he thought. *Too close.*

As Sebastian got up, he realized that he had something in one paw. It was Emily's map of Central Park. He had been holding it for her.

Sebastian dusted himself off–at least the parts that he could reach. Then he opened the map. "I wonder where I am," he said. "And where I should go."

Suddenly, he remembered what Ms. Valentine had said. Mr. and Mrs. Parker would be at the zoo by 5 o'clock. *So I have to be there by then, too,* Sebastian realized. *I can do that.*

Sebastian studied the map. "Zoo" was a word he knew. So he was able to find it on the map. That told him where he was going. But he still didn't know where he was.

Sebastian folded the map and tucked it into his backpack. "I'll figure it out somehow," he said bravely, looking around. "I know I will."

Despite his words, Sebastian was worried. He looked down the path, hoping that Emily had noticed he was missing. Maybe she was already on the way to rescue him.

People zoomed by on bicycles, skateboards, scooters, and in-line skates. They walked, skipped, and ran. But none of them was Emily.

Well, if I don't get started, I'll never get there, Sebastian decided. *But I think I'll be safer if I stay off the path.*

Zoom! A skateboarder passed so close that the wheels just missed Sebastian!

Sebastian started walking in the grass. It was a lot slower than riding. It was a lot hotter, too. Before long, he was thirsty.

"Maybe I'll find another pond," he said out loud, to give himself courage. "One with no turtles."

Before long, Sebastian heard a wonderful sound. It was water! He climbed up on a bench at the edge of the path. In the distance, he could see water spraying into the air.

"A fountain!" he cried.

Sebastian climbed down and started across the path in the direction of the fountain. Zoom! A skateboarder passed so close that the wheels just missed Sebastian! The bear jumped back and landed on his rear end.

As he got back up, Sebastian remembered what Ms. Valentine always told Ben and Emily. "Look both ways before you cross," he said aloud.

Sebastian looked one way, then the other. At last, there was no one coming in either direction. He hurried across as fast as his furry legs could take him. Then he made his way through the grassy field to the fountain.

As he got closer, a wet mist fogged up his sunglasses. The cool water felt so good. Sebastian was sure it would taste even better.

He leaned over the edge of the pool. Then he wiggled forward, trying to get his mouth close enough for a drink.

The next thing Sebastian knew, he was falling. *I wish I knew how to swim*, he thought frantically.

Chapter Six
Sebastian Meets a Hero

Once again, Sebastian found himself lifted into the air. *It's Emily*, he thought. *She came back to rescue me!*

But Sebastian found himself hugged against an unfamiliar chest. Hugged much too tightly–and by hands that were very sticky.

"Mommy! I found a bear," a high voice cried. Sebastian was in the arms of a small boy. And it wasn't Ben.

"Put that thing down right now!" a woman said. She grabbed Sebastian from the little boy's arms.

"But I want him!" whined the child.

"You have better bears than this at home," the woman said. She held Sebastian in one outstretched arm, as if she didn't want to touch him. "He's dirty and wet. And who knows where he came from?" She dropped Sebastian on the ground and marched her son off.

"Dirty?" said Sebastian indignantly. Then he looked down at his clothing. *I suppose I am dirty,* he thought as he got up. *But it's hard for a little bear to stay clean when he's all by himself.*

For the first time, Sebastian began to feel scared. What if he didn't reach the zoo in time? What if he never saw Emily and Ben again? A tear trickled down his cheek.

Sebastian wiped the tear away, leaving another dirty streak on his face. *No use in crying,* he told himself. *I have to be brave. Otherwise, I'll be lost forever.*

Sebastian pulled the map out of his backpack and studied it again. There was the fountain. And there was the zoo. With the tip of one paw, he traced a path from one to the other. Then he tucked the map away and started out.

Sebastian walked and walked. He was tired and hungry and lonely. But he kept on going. Skateboarders and in-line skaters zoomed past. *I wish I could go that fast*, thought Sebastian. *I'd be at the zoo in no time.*

Then a skateboard screeched to a halt right beside him. Its rider scooted the board over to a drinking fountain and bent down to drink.

I could hitch a ride! thought Sebastian. As quietly as possible, he climbed on the back of the board. The skateboarder didn't notice. She finished her drink, then shoved off.

Sebastian flattened himself across the back of the board, his paws curled around its edges. They went up hills and down. They weaved in and out among other skaters, cyclists, and runners.

This is perfect! thought Sebastian. *I'll be at the zoo in no time.*

Then the skateboard flew into the air! Sebastian held on tighter! The board twisted, tilted, and headed back toward the ground.

Sebastian closed his eyes. He felt the skateboard crash to earth. His paws came loose, and he rolled across the path and into a bush.

Sebastian felt something grab the fur at the back of his neck.

Sebastian sat up and started picking leaves and twigs from his fur. "I guess bears aren't supposed to skateboard," he mumbled.

Suddenly, something wet and sloppy hit Sebastian hard on the back. He fell forward, his face in the dirt.

"Hey, I'm sorry," a gruff voice said. Sebastian felt something grab the fur at the back of his neck. Then he was hanging in the air.

"Put me down!" he yelled.

"Okay, okay! No need to shout," the voice said. Sebastian found himself on the ground again. He sat up and turned around.

A dog sat there beside him. A huge dog.

"Sorry," the dog said again. "I didn't mean to upset you. My name's Bernie, by the way."

"That's okay," Sebastian sighed. "I'm Sebastian."

Bernie raised a leg to scratch behind his ear. "You don't seem very happy. What's the matter?" he asked.

Sebastian looked into Bernie's big, brown eyes. The huge dog really seemed to care. So Sebastian found himself telling the whole story.

"No problem," Bernie said when Sebastian was finished. "I'll take you to the zoo."

"Do you know the way?" Sebastian asked.

"Know the way?" Bernie repeated. "I'm a New Yorker. I come here every time I can run away–I mean, whenever I can. I know every fountain and flower. Every statue and sidewalk. Every–"

"Okay," said Sebastian. "I believe you."

"Let's get moving," Bernie said. "I don't like to stay in one place too long. Some people don't think dogs should be on their own."

The dog opened his huge mouth to grab Sebastian by the back of the neck again. Sebastian backed away. The thought of being drooled on didn't appeal to him.

"Can I ride on your back instead?" he asked.

"I guess so," said Bernie.

The dog was so big that Sebastian had to ask him to lie down. Then he clambered up and grabbed hold of Bernie's collar.

The ride was bumpy–kind of like a rodeo ride, Sebastian imagined. And Sebastian soon discovered that Bernie had no intention of going directly to the zoo. No, he stopped every few feet to sniff something interesting. Or to scratch at the dirt. Or to drink from the puddles that formed under every drinking fountain.

"Hey, here's one of my favorite places," Bernie announced, stopping yet again. Sebastian wanted to beg the dog to keep on going, but something in Bernie's voice told him that this stop was important.

Bernie's eyes were fastened on a statue of a large dog. "He's my hero," Bernie said.

"Who is he?" Sebastian asked.

"Balto," said Bernie, as if the name should mean something to Sebastian.

"Who's Balto? And why is there a statue of him here?"

Bernie turned to stare at Sebastian. "You've never heard of Balto?" he asked. "Why, he saved hundreds of lives. He's one of the bravest dogs that ever lived."

Then Bernie told Balto's story. How the sled dog had helped to carry medicine across Alaska so that sick children wouldn't die.

"I wish I could be a hero," Bernie said sadly when his story was done. "But I never will be."

"Me, either," said Sebastian. "I've been trying to be brave. But before you found me, I was really scared."

"Well," said Bernie, still staring at the statue, "not everyone can be like Balto, I guess." Then he turned to Sebastian. "Come on," he said. "Let's get you to the zoo."

Bernie didn't stop again until they reached the gate of the zoo. "This is as far as I can go—they don't let dogs in here," he explained. "I'm not sure how they feel about bears," he added, "but since you're not a real bear, it'll probably be okay. Just be careful, will you?"

"I will," Sebastian promised. He looked up at his new friend. "May I take your picture?"

"A picture of me?" Bernie asked, suddenly looking shy. "Why would you want one?"

"Because you are a hero. My hero. You saved me when I was lost."

"Gosh," said Bernie. "Thanks."

Sebastian took out his camera, and Bernie struck a brave pose. Then the two friends said good-bye. Bernie ran off, his head held high.

Sebastian looked up at the big clock near the zoo entrance. It was only 4 o'clock. He was on time!

Chapter Seven
Monkey Business

Sebastian waited until a group of people were going though the gate. He scooted inside with them. No one looked down, so no one noticed him.

I'd better look for my family in case they got here before me, he thought. He began to wander around, looking for Emily and Ben and Ms. Valentine.

First he went into the gift shop. He knew that Ben would want to check that out. The shop was filled with interesting things. Sebastian saw posters and puppets and animal noses that he would have loved to try on. There were even lots of stuffed animals. *I wonder if any of them are real?* he thought. *Probably not. Not until they belong to someone who loves them.*

There was no sign of his family in the shop. So Sebastian went outside and began to wander through the zoo. He spent a long time watching the polar bears and penguins. He even tried walking like a penguin, but kept tripping over his own paws.

At last, Sebastian reached the rain forest exhibit. *Maybe Emily and Ben are in here,* he thought. It was hot inside. Tall trees towered overhead. The air was filled with the noise of waterfalls, birdsong, and monkey chatter.

Sebastian stopped to watch some monkeys. They were jumping and playing and swinging by their tails. *I wish I could do that,* he thought.

Then Sebastian noticed a zoo worker heading his way. The man had a bucket in one hand. It was feeding time for the monkeys!

The thought made Sebastian's tummy rumble. He hadn't eaten anything for hours. *I'll bet there are bananas in that bucket,* thought Sebastian. *Everyone knows that monkeys love bananas. And*

I'll bet that they wouldn't mind sharing.

So when the man opened the door, Sebastian slipped through behind him. He hid under a tall fern and watched.

The man put down the bucket and reached for a hose. He started to wash the floor. Sebastian edged closer to the bucket. *Just one banana*, he thought. But when he looked inside, there were no bananas. Just something that looked like breakfast cereal.

"Well," Sebastian whispered to himself, "if monkeys can eat it, I guess I can, too." He grabbed a pawful of food. Then he took a taste.

"Hmmm—not bad," he added and reached in again.

Soon Sebastian was busy eating. That's why he didn't notice when a monkey came over to check out her dinner. He didn't notice a thing until the monkey grabbed him by one leg!

"Help!" Sebastian cried. But the zoo worker didn't hear him.

Thumpety-bumpety—the monkey dragged Sebastian over the ground. Then she started to climb a tree.

He grabbed a pawful of food. Then he took a taste.

"Oh, help!" cried Sebastian as his head banged against the tree trunk. But the monkey kept going. Sebastian closed his eyes tightly.

At last, they stopped moving. Sebastian opened one eye, then the other. He was 15 feet off the ground, dangling head first. He felt dizzy.

Finally, the monkey pulled Sebastian up to the safety of a branch. The bear scooted backward until he could feel the tree trunk. The monkey grinned at him.

"I'm a bear," said Sebastian. "I don't belong in a monkey cage."

"My bear," said the monkey.

"No!" cried Sebastian. "I belong to Emily and Ben!"

"My bear," the monkey repeated. Then she turned her back on Sebastian and started scratching herself.

How rude, thought Sebastian. But he had bigger things to worry about than the monkey's manners. How would Emily and Ben find him now? How was he going to get out of this mess?

Chapter Eight
Sebastian Saves the Day

After a while, Sebastian thought about climbing down. But as soon as he moved, the monkey grabbed him and jumped to another branch.

So Sebastian sat very still. He thought about Emily and Ben and how much he was going to miss them. He thought about pancakes and honey and how he'd never eat them again.

Sebastian was tired, but he didn't dare nap. If he fell asleep, he might tumble out of the tree. Even being stuffed wouldn't save him then. He'd fall into the huge pool of water directly under the tree.

Sebastian was about to burst into tears when he saw something below—something familiar. It was Emily! And Ben and Ms. Valentine were with her. His whole family was here! He had found them!

But could they find him? Sebastian wound one arm around the branch. He leaned forward, and shouted as loudly as he could: "Emily! Ben! I'm up here! Up in the tree!"

They couldn't hear him, Sebastian realized. Not with all the chattering monkeys. He had to climb down closer to them. He had to!

But as soon as Sebastian started to move, the monkey grabbed him by one paw and took a great leap through the air.

"Help!" screamed Sebastian.

The monkey leaped again. And again.

Then Sebastian realized something. With each leap, they were getting closer to the ground.

The monkey stopped at last. She wound her longs arms around Sebastian. Then she twisted her tail around a branch. In seconds, she was swinging—and so was Sebastian.

Emily and Ben were right below. Sebastian could hear Ms. Valentine telling them all about the

In seconds, she was swinging–and so was Sebastian.

monkeys. But the children weren't paying much attention.

At last, Ms. Valentine finished and said, "Well, it's almost time to go."

"We can't," Emily said. She sounded like she was close to tears.

"Emily's right," Ben added. "We have to find Sebastian."

"I'm sorry," said Ms. Valentine. "But we've already wasted the entire afternoon looking for him. There is so much about this wonderful park that you didn't learn." She pulled her schedule from her shoulder bag. Sebastian noticed that the paper was still crisp and white.

Ms. Valentine shook her head. In a sad voice, she said, "I wanted you to see the Discovery Center. We could have taken a nature tour there. And the Boathouse–you should have seen that. There is so much to learn in this park, and we missed half of it."

She sighed and returned the schedule to her bag. "Well, no use in crying over a ruined schedule, I suppose. Your parents will be here in a few minutes. We have to head to the airport."

"But Sebastian has to come with us!" Emily wailed.

Sebastian tried to call out to her. But the monkey's arm was across his mouth, so all that came out was "Emmmmm!"

Then Sebastian had an idea. He reached for the strap of his sunglasses. With some difficulty, he managed to pull it over his head. Then, as the monkey swung over Emily, Sebastian dropped the sunglasses.

"What?" cried Emily when something bounced off her head. She looked up. "Sebastian!"

"A monkey's got him!" Ben shouted.

"Nonsense," said Ms. Valentine. Then she looked up, too. "My goodness! It *is* Sebastian!"

"We have to save him!" cried Emily.

"Let's not panic, Emily," said Ms. Valentine. "I'll take care of this, or my name's not Arabella Valentine." She marched off, returning in a few minutes with a zoo worker.

"A bear?" the worker was saying in a puzzled voice.

"Yes," said Ms. Valentine. "A stuffed bear. Your monkey has him."

The man stared up at Sebastian and the monkey. He scratched his head. "Hmmm," he said at last. "You're not supposed to throw things into the monkey exhibit, children."

"We didn't," said Emily.

"Can you rescue him?" Ben asked.

The man scratched his head again, then nodded. "Wait here," he said.

The man unlocked the door and entered the exhibit. Then he pulled a banana from his pocket. "Come on, Princess," he called. "I have a nice treat for you."

For one horrible moment, Sebastian thought that Princess might not like bananas. But then she stopped swinging. She pulled herself up on the branch and scampered toward the zoo worker.

At the same time, she dropped Sebastian. He landed on his head in a big bush.

But a moment later, the zoo worker handed Sebastian to Emily.

"Oh, Sebastian," she said. "I was afraid I'd never see you again."

"I was afraid, too," whispered Sebastian. He

snuggled happily in Emily's arms.

The children thanked the zoo worker. He warned them to keep track of their things.

Then Ms. Valentine shook her head and sighed loudly. "Well," she said, "the day has certainly not gone as planned. We never got to see the Boathouse. And we never got to see the statue of Balto. Now, that is a story you could have learned something from." She sighed again and walked off. "Come, children, we have to be at the gate in five minutes."

"Balto?" echoed Sebastian. "Did she say Balto?"

"Yes," said Emily.

Sebastian started to whisper to Emily and Ben. He told them all about Bernie, and about Balto.

"Ms. Valentine, wait!" Emily called. She and Ben ran to catch up.

"What is it?"

"Well, I just wanted to say that we do know the story of Balto," said Emily. "And you're right, he was a hero."

"How do you know the story?" Ms. Valentine asked.

"Oh, a friend told us," said Ben.

Ms. Valentine smiled. Then she started asking questions. And telling them more about Balto and the other sled dogs that had helped carry medicine across Alaska.

"So, you can see why they were heroes," Ms. Valentine said, finishing her story. "They didn't give up. No matter what happened, they kept on going."

"That's a wonderful story," said Emily. Then she whispered in Sebastian's ear, "You're a hero, too, Sebastian."

"I don't think so," the little bear said sadly. "I

was scared. I even cried once."

"But you didn't give up when you were scared," Emily said. "You kept going–just like Balto. And you figured out how to save yourself."

"Well," said Sebastian, "I did have some help."

"Hurry!" Ms. Valentine said suddenly. "I see your parents. Just think, children, by morning we'll be in London."

London! Sebastian thought. *I can't wait to see what happens there!*

EXPLORING CENTRAL PARK

By Emily Parker

Central Park is one of the most famous parks in the world–and a really amazing place. It was built more than 100 years ago as a place where New Yorkers could take a break from their busy lives and escape the noise of the city.

Today, millions of visitors from all over the world–like Ms. Valentine, Ben, Sebastian, and me!–come to Central Park to have fun and visit special places inside it, such as the Children's Zoo and Belvedere Castle. What I liked best was being in a great big, open space filled with nature – while at the same time being surrounded by huge skyscrapers! What a strange feeling!

Emily Parker's
TOP 5
Most Interesting Things About New York City (NYC)

ILOVE New York!

1 8,000,000 people live in NYC.

2 More than 30 million tourists visit NYC every year. *(not counting bears!)*

3 NYC used to be five separate cities (they joined together in 1898).

4 There are 150 museums in NYC!

5 NYC used to be the U.S. Capital (1789-1790).

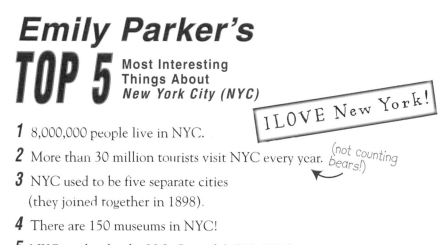

The five original cities became what are now called the five "boroughs" of New York City:

The Bronx   Brooklyn   Manhattan   Queens   Staten Island

This is where Central Park is.

NYC has lots of interesting places to visit.

The Statue of Liberty is one of my favorite places in New York. It was a gift from the people of France, honoring the 100th birthday of the Declaration of Independence. Did you know that she is 305 feet tall, and one of her fingers is eight feet long?

Ellis Island was a U.S. government station where people from other nations first entered this country. More than 12 million people passed through its doors between the 1890s and 1930s. These people were called "immigrants" and most of them became American citizens. Now it's a national park with interesting exhibits about the immigrants and their experiences.

hmmm—I wonder how many bears came to Ellis Island?

The History of Central Park

The story of Central Park began in the 1850s with a new idea. New York was growing very quickly, and many people who lived there wanted to escape the noise and crowds of city life.

The new idea was to set aside a piece of land as a public park–a place where everyone could enjoy nature and open space. This was a new idea, because before then, nearly all parks were for private homes, businesses, or clubs. Lots of people didn't have a park they could use.

The city obtained 843 acres of land for its new park and held a contest to design it. The winners were Frederick Law Olmsted and Calvert Vaux, and their plan was called the Greensward Plan. They were inspired by many gardens and parks in England.

Central Park used to be blocks away from the busy city. Less than a million people lived in New York when the park was built. Today, New York has 8 million people, and the park has busy streets and tall buildings right next to it!

Work on Central Park began in 1858 and lasted for almost 20 years. It was a big job. More than 5 million cubic feet of topsoil, stone, and earth were moved into the park, and 4 million new plants, trees, and shrubs were planted. More than 30 bridges were built, and four man-made lakes and ponds were created. Thousands of people were needed to do all the work!

What's In Central Park?

- 26,000 trees
- 8,968 benches
- 275 kinds of birds
- 250 acres of lawn
- 21 playgrounds
- 7 bodies of water
- and lots more!

54

Favorite Places

There are 51 fountains, monuments, and sculptures in Central Park. Some are war memorials.

Some honor famous people, or dogs! such as Hans Christian Anderson, and Balto. Others honor famous events, such as Columbus' arrival in the Americas.

Cleopatra's Needle

This is the oldest statue in Central Park—it's 3,600 years old! It was built in 1,500 BC in Egypt and given as a gift to the United States in 1879. Its real name is the "The Obelisk," and it doesn't really have anything to do with Cleopatra.

The Obelisk is 70 feet high and weighs almost 250 tons!

Statue of Balto

This statue is one of the most popular in Central Park. Balto was a hero who led a dogsled team through an Alaskan blizzard to deliver medicine to sick children. The real Balto actually visited Central Park for the dedication of his statue!

Way too high for a little bear to climb!

55

More Sites to Visit in Central Park

Bethesda Fountain

This was the only sculpture in the original plan for Central Park. It is also called "Angel of the Waters" and was built in honor of an aqueduct that brought fresh drinking water to New York beginning in 1842. An aqueduct is a channel or special system that carries water from one place to another.

Did you know that NYC uses 1.3 billion gallons of water each day?

The Children's Zoo

Everyone calls it the Children's Zoo, but its real name is the Central Park Wildlife Center. More than 1,400 animals live here, including sea lions, penguins, polar bears, and even monkeys.

Monkeys are definitely NOT Sebastian's favorite animals.

Belvedere Castle

The Henry Luce Observatory, inside the castle, is a cool place where you can learn how scientists study nature. I liked looking at things through the microscopes and listening to recordings of real bird songs. Special weather instruments at the castle have been collecting weather data since 1919! It's one of the oldest weather stations in the U.S.

Turtle Pond

There's an island in the middle of Turtle Pond where turtles lay eggs and birds build nests. There is even a nature blind so that you can see them close-up! Sometimes, turtles sun themselves on dead tree trunks on the island.

Important note: Because of all the turtles, this may not be the best place to bring small, curious bears!

Fun Facts

Central Park is completely man-made.

More than 150 movies have scenes filmed in Central Park.

Some rocks in Central Park are 450 million years old.

20 million people visit Central Park each year.

There are 58 miles of paths in Central Park.

Remember to hold on to small bears so they don't get lost!

Birds In Central Park

Some of the most common summer birds are:

American robin
black-capped chickadee
Northern cardinal
mallard duck
European starling
ruby-throated hummingbird

Central Park is one of the best places in the U.S. for bird-watching. More than 270 species of birds have been seen in the park. Many of them are migratory birds that stop in the park on their travels north or south.

Later!

Special thanks to the Central Park Conservancy,
a private not-for-profit organization that manages Central
Park. They provided photos and background information used
in *Exploring Central Park*.

bear& company™

IF YOU ENJOYED this book,
you'll find lots more to love in
the Bear & Company catalog.

With a little magic and
make-believe, even the
littlest bear can do amazing things! A great family
read-aloud. *Recommended
for ages 3–6.*

Follow a trio of animal
detectives as they solve
mysteries in their forest
home. A great choice
for young readers! *Recommended
for ages 5–9.*

Discover some of the
world's most interesting
habitats through the
adventures of animals that
live there. *Recommended
for ages 4–10.*

A teddy bear travels the
globe and finds mischief
and fun wherever he
goes. Lots of fun for
chapter book readers who love travel
adventures. *Recommended for ages 6–10.*

Three easy ways to request a free catalog
◆ *Mail the postcard below*
◆ *Visit www.BearandCo.com*
◆ *Call 1-800-596-4577*

Please send me a catalog!

I'm interested in: (check all that apply)

☐ Digby in Disguise   ☐ My Home
☐ Duke The Bear Detective   ☐ Suitcase Bear Adventures

Name _____

Address _____

City _____ State _____ Zip _____

Email Address _____
Please provide email address if you are 18 or older and interested in receiving email updates from Bear & Company.

Send a catalog to my friend!

Name _____

Address _____

City _____ State _____ Zip _____

bear& company™

IF THE POSTCARD below has already been used and you would like a Bear & Company catalog, send your name and address to:

Bear & Company
P.O. Box 3876
Gettysburg, PA 17325

OR visit us on the web at
www.BearandCo.com

OR call 1 800-596-4577

Stories to inspire your imagination . . .
. . . New friends to warm your heart™